NOBODY ASKED THE PEA

by John Warren Stewig

illustrated by Cornelius Van Wright

Holiday House / New York

To Barbara J. Michaels and to Patricia Basich,
each a volunteer extraordinaire who has helped
our center thrive.   J. W. S.

To Nanette & Gary. Live Happily Ever After.
                                        C. V. W.

Text copyright © 2013 by John Warren Stewig
Illustrations copyright © 2013 by Cornelius Van Wright
All Rights Reserved
HOLIDAY HOUSE is registered in the U.S. Patent and Trademark Office.
Printed and Bound in October 2012 at Toppan Leefung, DongGuan City, China.
The text typefaces are Agenda, Alghera, Auldroon, Bernhard Modern, Birdlegs,
Centaur, Dolly, Hank, Happy, Moonbeam, Pink Martini, and Shannon Book.
The art for this book was created in watercolors and pencil on Strathmore Board.
www.holidayhouse.com
First Edition
1 3 5 7 9 10 8 6 4 2

Library of Congress Cataloging-in-Publication Data
Stewig, John Warren.
Nobody asked the pea / by John Warren Stewig ; illustrated by Cornelius Van Wright. — 1st ed.
p. cm.
Summary: Expands upon the classic tale of the princess and the pea as seen through the eyes
of the prince, the princess, the king and queen, various servants, a mouse, and even the rather vain pea, itself.
ISBN 978-0-8234-2224-1 (hardcover)
[1. Princesses—Fiction. 2. Princes—Fiction. 3. Kings, queens, rulers, etc.—Fiction. 4. Stories in rhyme.
5. Mice—Fiction.] I. Van Wright, Cornelius, ill. II. Title.
PZ8.S64Nob 2012
[E]—dc23
2011024048

Princess
Lucy

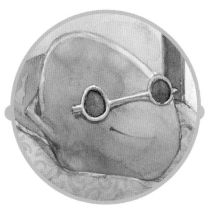
Patrick,
the Pea

Queen
Mildred

Prince Harold

THE CAST OF CHARACTERS

Princess Lucy's Page

Roger,
the Doorman

Mother Mouse

King Henry

The New Head Housekeeper

Maribeth,
Princess Tina's Maid

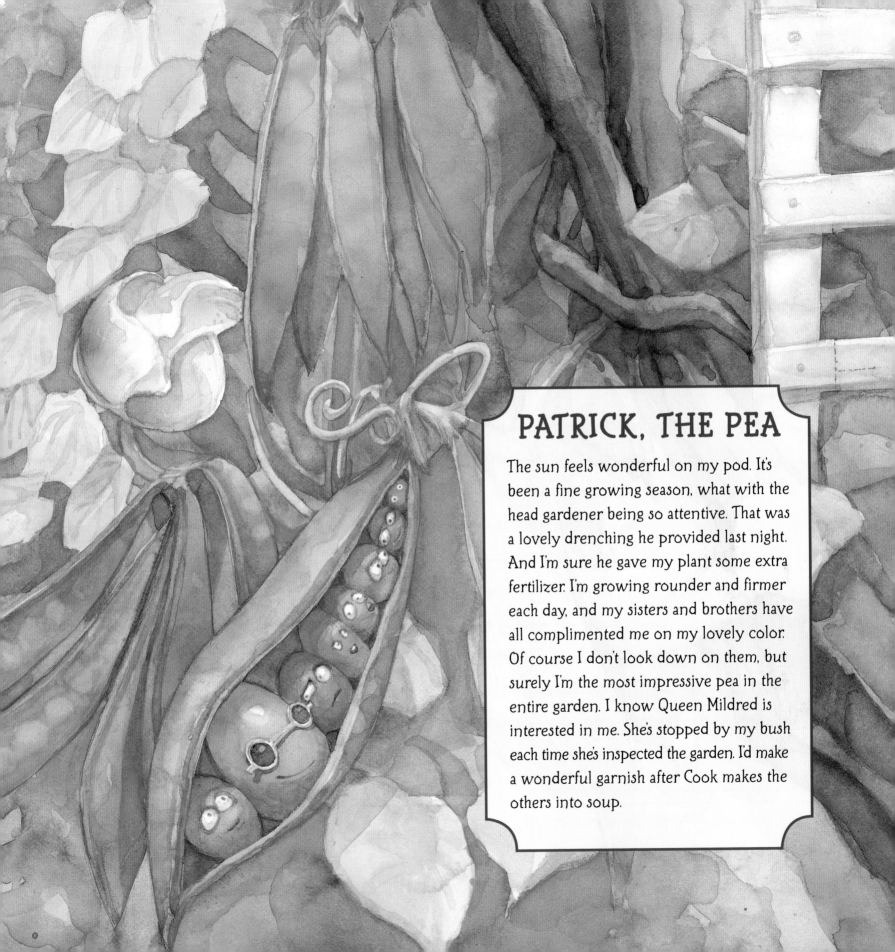

PATRICK, THE PEA

The sun feels wonderful on my pod. It's been a fine growing season, what with the head gardener being so attentive. That was a lovely drenching he provided last night. And I'm sure he gave my plant some extra fertilizer. I'm growing rounder and firmer each day, and my sisters and brothers have all complimented me on my lovely color. Of course I don't look down on them, but surely I'm the most impressive pea in the entire garden. I know Queen Mildred is interested in me. She's stopped by my bush each time she's inspected the garden. I'd make a wonderful garnish after Cook makes the others into soup.

QUEEN MILDRED

I'm determined, Harold. We've talked about this as each of those prior princesses has visited, and my mind is made up. It is far past time for you to choose a wife. The page has returned from King Timothy's palace saying that they are expecting you. His daughter, Princess Tina, is a lovely young child, or I've been told. After you've had a pleasant visit there, you just haul her back here, and I can determine if she is suitable for you. No, I won't tell you my plan. Just make things ready for your journey.

What will the other royalty think if you continue this lollygagging? All the other princes are long since married. Several, I hasten to point out, have already gifted their mothers with lovely grandchildren. After all your father and I have done for you. . . . Don't interrupt, Henry. Just saying "Yes, dear" is quite sufficient.

PRINCE HAROLD

Why should I marry? Just consider this, Edgar. I have the run of a lovely palace, attentive servants such as you to cater to my every need, a forest to hunt in, and parents who aren't too bothersome. Most of the time, anyway. Who could want for more?

Yes, you will need to pack my second best crown. That's certainly good enough for this Princess Tina, whoever she is. There's a forecast of rain, and moisture always tarnishes the best one. Just in case this Tina person turns out to be acceptable, we need to make a fine impression. Why Mother wants me to drag her back here for a visit before the betrothal, I don't understand. Seems quite good enough for her to stay in her own palace until the wedding, if there is to be one. Of course, if she turns out to be a huntswoman, she might pass muster.

MOTHER MOUSE

No, my dears. You can't come along to breakfast with me. As soon as I can, I'll bring back treats. Yes, there was quite a large wedge of that delicious imported Camembert last night, and I know how fond you are of that. This castle has always had high-quality crumbs.

But I've heard that new head housekeeper stomping around. She's a terror, that one is. Old Mrs. Mortimor's sight was so bad, she was never a danger. Now we must be more careful.

On top of that, the servants are all scurrying around setting things to rights, as Prince Harold is soon returning with another of those princesses. With all the flurry, you might be trod upon. So until I get back, remember, "Out of sight, out of mind."

MARIBETH, PRINCESS TINA'S MAID

Oh, Princess, he's lovely to look at! I know I shouldn't say anything, but he does look right handsome and very athletic, though I hope for your sake he doesn't spend all his time outdoors. You'd not like that, I know.

Yes, ma'am, I'll lay out the yellow taffeta gown. Indeed you're right that it does bring out the lovely green in your eyes. So clever of you to have created it yourself. I think that of all the dresses you've designed, I like this one the best.

Oh, do you think he'll propose soon? I know I wasn't supposed to be listening, but I heard your father and Prince Harold talking in the library about you making a visit to meet Queen Mildred and King Henry. Oh, ma'am, you'll take me with you? I'd love that, but how will I ever pack all the dresses you'll need for such a visit?

THE NEW HEAD HOUSEKEEPER

Come along, girl. We've much to do before Prince Harold and Princess Tina arrive. Get a few of the other girls. Do you see this pile of mattresses? They must all be moved up into the guest room immediately. Why are we doing this? Never you mind. Yes, I know they're heavy and awkward, which is why you'll need extra help.

Yes, you may take them up the public stair, since no one is here except us. King Henry and Prince Harold are out tramping around in the forest, as always, so there will be muddy boots in the hallway again. I don't know where Queen Mildred has got to. And mind, after you've finished, I want no talk in the servants' quarters.

QUEEN MILDRED

My, the garden is looking particularly productive. Obviously the gardener has been following my instructions. It puts other palace gardens to shame. Queen Alice can't grow anything but weeds, and Queen Margaret's peas always look scraggly.

This pea plant seems especially sturdy. I'll just pick off the biggest pod and get back into the castle before the housekeeper finishes supervising placing the mattresses. She's a nosy one, she is, and I don't want her to know about my plan. But she's efficient, and every servant has some drawback or other. Isn't that true, Henry?

KING HENRY

Yes, dear. But why you want that stack of mattresses on the bed in the guest suite is beyond me. I had to call for a ladder so that poor Tina could climb into bed. She seems like a sweet little thing. She protested that heights make her dizzy, but once you decide something, it's decided.

Perhaps when all this foolish marrying business is settled, I can go back to hunting more than twice a week. The stable master told me of a huge stag in our woods, and I know I just get underfoot when you're overseeing matters in the castle.

ROGER, THE DOORMAN

How that poor man does it is beyond me. He's been married to her for nearly a quarter century, and how she does go on, continually. Lucky he has me. Of course, strictly speaking, it isn't a doorman's job to tend horses and ride with a king. But he's a good chap who needs a listening ear most days.

And there goes the queen again, into the garden, probably to rag on the gardener. She just finished dressing down the housekeeper because the tracks Prince Harold left on the hall floor weren't wiped up yet. Can't seem to understand that when men come home from hunting, there's bound to be a little mud.

MOTHER MOUSE

Children, you'll never believe the conversation at breakfast, which is why I have to tell you. Such interesting stories can be learned from under the sideboard. First off, Queen Mildred was at the head of the table before the sun was even up. And then King Henry and Prince Harold straggled in, so late the coffee was cold. Last of all was Princess Tina, and did she look a sight! She was all primped and powdered. In a different gown than she wore last night, as is only proper. Queen Mildred asked her how she had slept, and she smiled sweetly and said, "Like a log." So unladylike!

Well, then the conversation stopped about dead. Nothing much happened after that except eating, until Queen Mildred announced Princess Tina would be returning home today. That poor maid she brought along had no more than gotten the four gowns unpacked, and now she's packing them all up again. That's a lot of work for naught. I guess there'll be no wedding for a while.

ROGER,
THE DOORMAN

Here we go again. Not to an exciting hunt, but on another journey. This time we're off to the palace of King Edgar and Queen Maude, and we're going to return Princess Margaret. Personally, though it's not my place, I thought she was a lovely young woman. Of course, I thought that about Princess Tina, and all the others before her too. I guess I'm just a pushover for a pretty face.

I'm fairly well worn-out, not being as young as I once was. Prince Harold is a considerate master, but I heard him telling the stable boy we're going on the path around the mountain, which is far longer. Couldn't be that he enjoys being away from his mother, could it?

PRINCE HAROLD

Dad, come over to the window and look. That's a fine horse, and the dogs are obviously purebred. Strange, there's a really disheveled woman dismounting. And she wasn't riding sidesaddle. Now look; despite the weather, she's stopped to give her dogs a scratch. That storm is so bad, we're lucky to be up here in the den and not underfoot with Mother storming around downstairs.

Wonder who she is? Oh, well, tomorrow morning is quite soon enough to meet her and find out where she gets her horses. It's clear she can't continue her journey in this weather. I think we should send for one of the maids to bring supper up here, don't you? And perhaps the stable boy could sneak our dogs up the back stair so they can have a nap before the fire. They deserve it.

ROGER, THE DOORMAN

You've never seen such a sight, my girl. Bring me some more warm wine while I toast my feet by the fire, and I'll tell you all the details. Such lightning and thunder I've never seen nor heard in all my days in these parts, and that's more than I can count. Thanks, deary. That spot of wine does my heart good.

At any rate, early evening, all of a sudden I heard a banging at the front door. I guess I had dozed a bit, door duty being tiresome and all. When I opened it, you should have seen the sight. This young girl was drenched to the skin, water dripping off her crown, down her neck, into her dress, all the way past I can't tell what, and running out into her shoes. Her page was as bedraggled as she was, and the horses were pawing the ground, glad to finally be out of the worst of the storm.

Well, the maids immediately bundled the woman up the public staircase because she insists she is a princess. She must be, because of the crown. Though I've never heard of her—Princess Lucy—nor the kingdom she says she's from. You can bet the queen looked her over a good one, what with Prince Harold still being unwed. They sent supper up to her, so that's the end of my tale.

PRINCESS LUCY

There's only one word for these sleeping arrangements, I'd say. Peculiar. Oh, the room is pleasant enough, and the maids are attentive; but who sleeps on such a mountain of mattresses? This climbing up a ladder to get into bed certainly isn't anything we do in our kingdom. That clock in the entry hall just banged again—it's three a.m. and I haven't slept. There's something under those mattresses, and I can't get comfortable enough to drift off—I'll look a proper sight when I go down to breakfast. What do you suppose that prince will think when I meet him? Worse yet, what will that dragon of a mother of his think? She was certainly unfriendly when I sloshed into her front hall.

Princess Lucy's Page

About drowned ourselves, we did. "Just another little adventure," the princess said, so off we went. Don't know why her parents let her go off with only me to attend her, but they want her independent, so they say. No daughter of mine would go so far from home. Lucky I don't have one. I take care of her as if she were my own. Oh, we've been here, there, and elsewhere; and usually it's all right with me. Makes for fine storytelling when I get back to the servants' quarters. This tale will certainly top old Ned's telling about falling into the river. Of course, I'd never tell the princess's mother or she'd think a second time about letting us go out.

It was a fine day for a ramble, until near sundown. And then that storm came up so unexpected and so fierce. The staff was pleasant enough when we washed into the receiving hall. But I don't trust that queen. She's a real dragon, despite her smile.

PATRICK, THE PEA

What a strange night I've had. First, the queen came into the garden during a storm like we've not had in an age. She's come before, only in fair weather, picked a single pea, and taken it away. This time she took only me. Of course, I am rounder, firmer, and a better color than the others. I know my brothers and sisters in the pod were disappointed, but it can't be helped.

Next, she took me straight up to the guest room, a strange destination. But why she put me under those mattresses and left me, I certainly don't know. To add insult to injury, when that princess got into bed, she didn't lie still a minute. No, it was toss here, turn there, roll somewhere else the whole night through. Why, it is a wonder I wasn't squashed flat. But I'm one tough pea, despite my pleasing appearance. She's finally gone downstairs, so I'll just have a little doze until . . .

MOTHER MOUSE

Now listen, you little rascals. Don't you want to hear the big news from upstairs? The queen was presiding as usual at the head of the table, with King Henry and Prince Harold wandering in later. Last of all, that woman who claims she's a princess came in. Well, of course, anyone could have nicked a crown, and maybe it isn't even real gold. The princess was a sight! Her eyes were red; there were big, black tiredness bags under them; and she dragged in, stretching and yawning like she hadn't slept a wink. Who could, with those dratted mattresses on the guest bed? She admitted as much when Queen Mildred asked her.

Now, here's the strange thing. When the girl said something under the mattresses had kept her awake all night, that delighted the queen. Odd! She jumped up and hugged the girl until she might have suffocated her. Now she's chattering away about wedding plans. Prince Harold and the king are looking bewildered, and the princess is just yawning with her chin drooping toward her chest.

And now I've got to go along. I believe some aged Swiss is waiting for us.

THE NEW HEAD HOUSEKEEPER

I swear to goodness, there are crumbs here, there, and everywhere. Things haven't been shipshape here in a while, despite the eagle eye that Queen Mildred keeps on every little thing. A castle this drafty and this wet must be full of mice, rats, and worse. Last night, we mopped up puddles from the latest princess. She's as muddy as the prince is. And this morning, a big piece of Swiss cheese the butler laid out disappeared before they all came down to breakfast.

As if daily doings aren't enough, keeping me and my girls hopping, now the queen announced there's to be a wedding. A big one, according to the talk. I swear I heard Queen Mildred mutter, "I'll show everyone who can give the best wedding." I already know what that means for me and my serving girls.

QUEEN MILDRED

What a pleasure having you here, dear sister. What an event I've planned! All the best people are here. Have you ever seen such gorgeous roses and gardenias? And the food! Oh, do try a pastry. We brought in extra girls from the village to help Cook, and they really outdid themselves. People will be talking about the wedding for decades, especially that dreadful Queen Estelle, who couldn't plan a trip to the privy by herself.

And it is clearly a marriage made in heaven, with considerable help from me, I might add. I'd really rather dear Lucy didn't smell of horse more often than necessary, but I can work on that when they're back from the honeymoon. And fancy, they're off hunting, at a spot she recommended. Not the way we did it in my time, I'd say, but we must keep up with the new ways. At least Harold is finally married, and I expect grandchildren will be on the way soon.

PRINCE HAROLD

Well, at least that's over. What a lot of fuss. Too much of everything. But that's the way Mother always insists on doing everything. Oh, no, no, no, my dear, you did look lovely. Not quite yourself in all that gown and veil. I quite loved you when I saw you at breakfast that first morning, even though you said how poorly you'd slept and that it made you look less than your best. Not a bit of it.

How delightful we're off on a hunting honeymoon, with you looking quite delectable in your riding habit. You say that forest three kingdoms away is your favorite spot? Then it will become my favorite, as well. I don't know how I was so lucky to get an outdoors girl who likes to hunt. We'll take the long way around the mountain, the better to enjoy the day.

PATRICK, THE PEA

It certainly isn't very exciting for a celebrity like me to be sitting here. Oh, indeed, my quarters are quite plush. I like the beveled glass; and the purple velvet is a good color for my complexion, and quite soft. The spotlight above my case is shining on my best side. All that's how it should be in a royal museum. The brass plaque tells the story of how I helped the queen select a bride for Prince Harold, though the crowds coming to see me have thinned out now that the wedding occurred nearly five years ago.

Queen Mother Mildred brought her grandchildren to see me, and they are cute little things. Good bloodline, that Queen Lucy. But time passes, and I'm getting more shriveled. I hope my grandchildren in the palace garden are hearing the story.

But more than that, who knows when one of them will be selected to help a queen pick a princess, or a prince. Even though Lucy and Harold's little girl, Rose, is only four years old, I heard Queen Mother Mildred telling her that someday her prince—a real one—will come along. I wonder. . . .